At the Vet

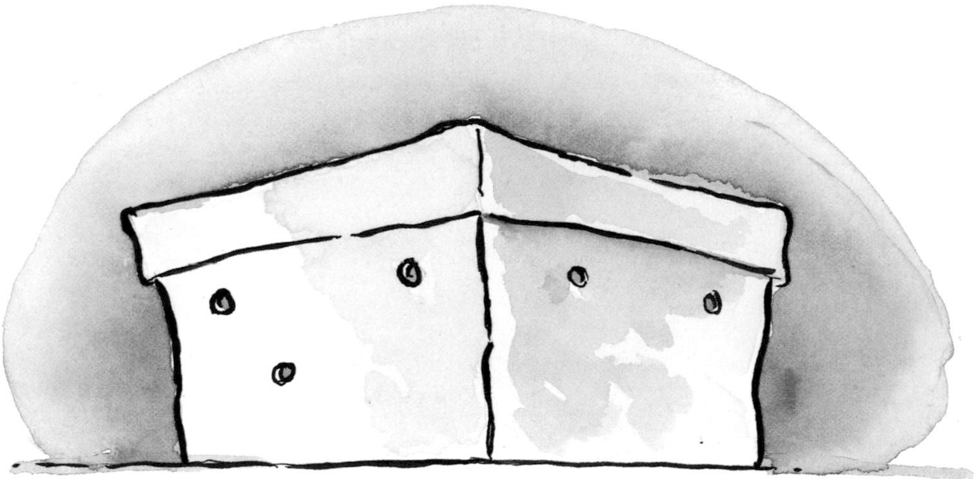

Monica Hughes
Illustrated by Michael Irwin

RIGBY

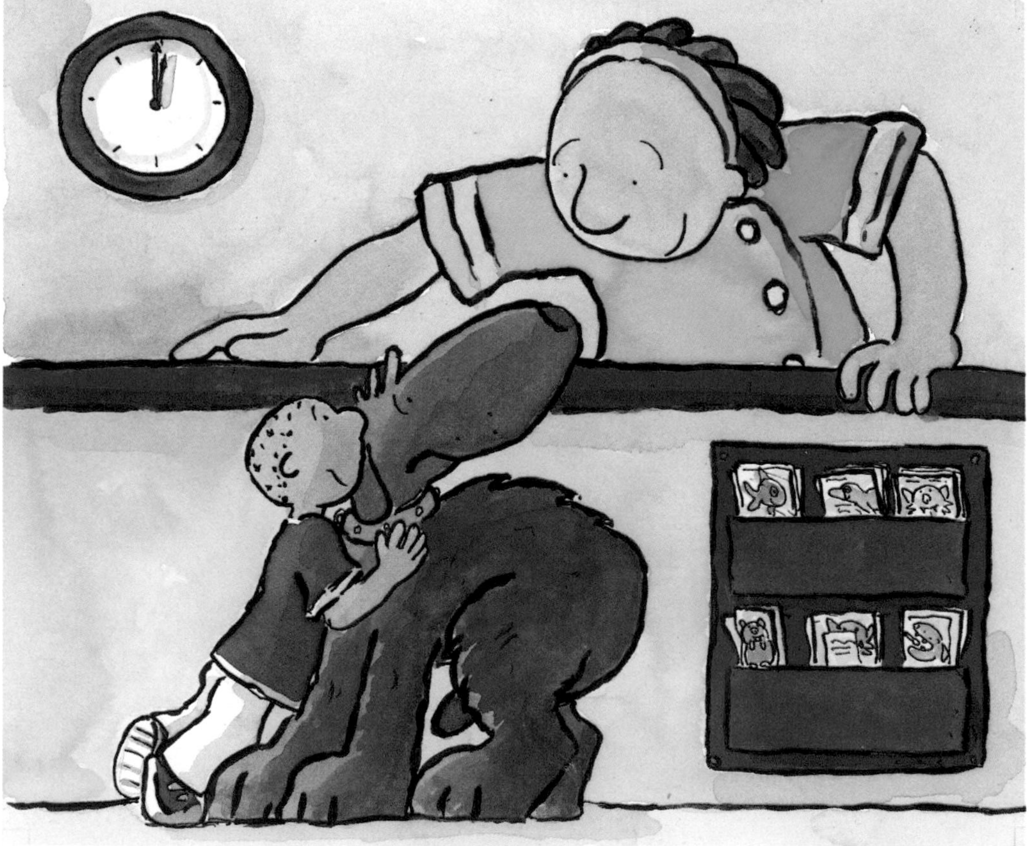

My pet is a dog.

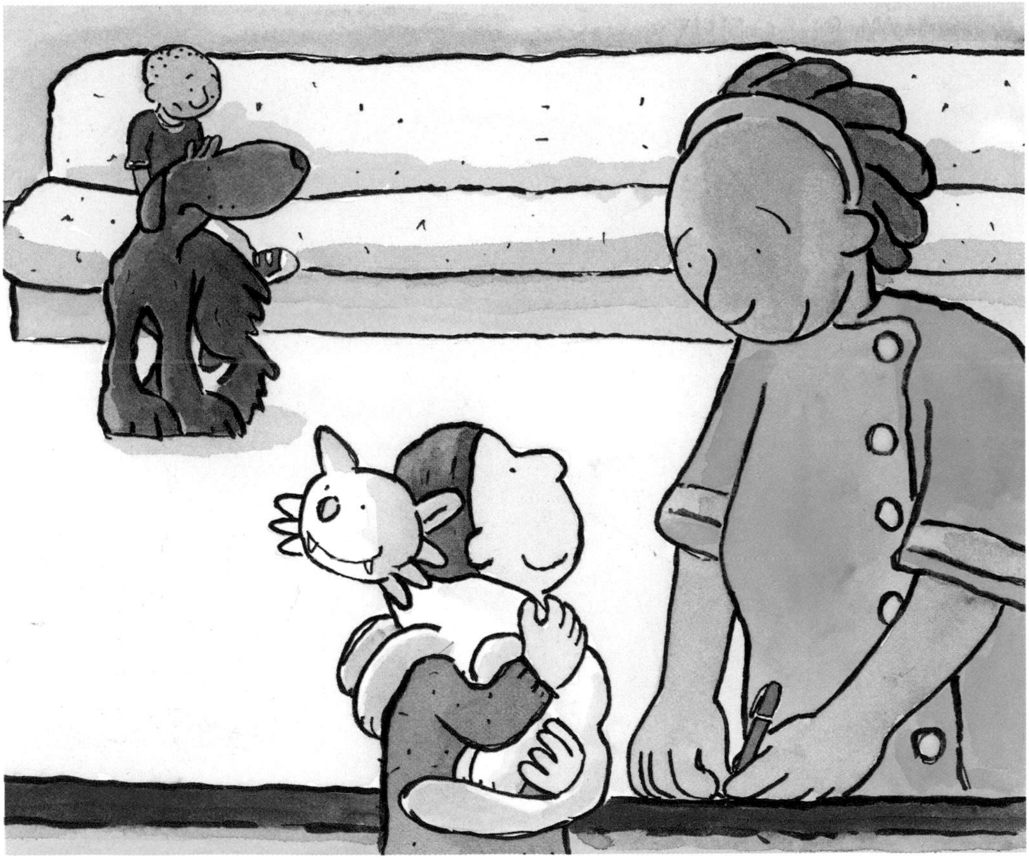

My pet is a cat.

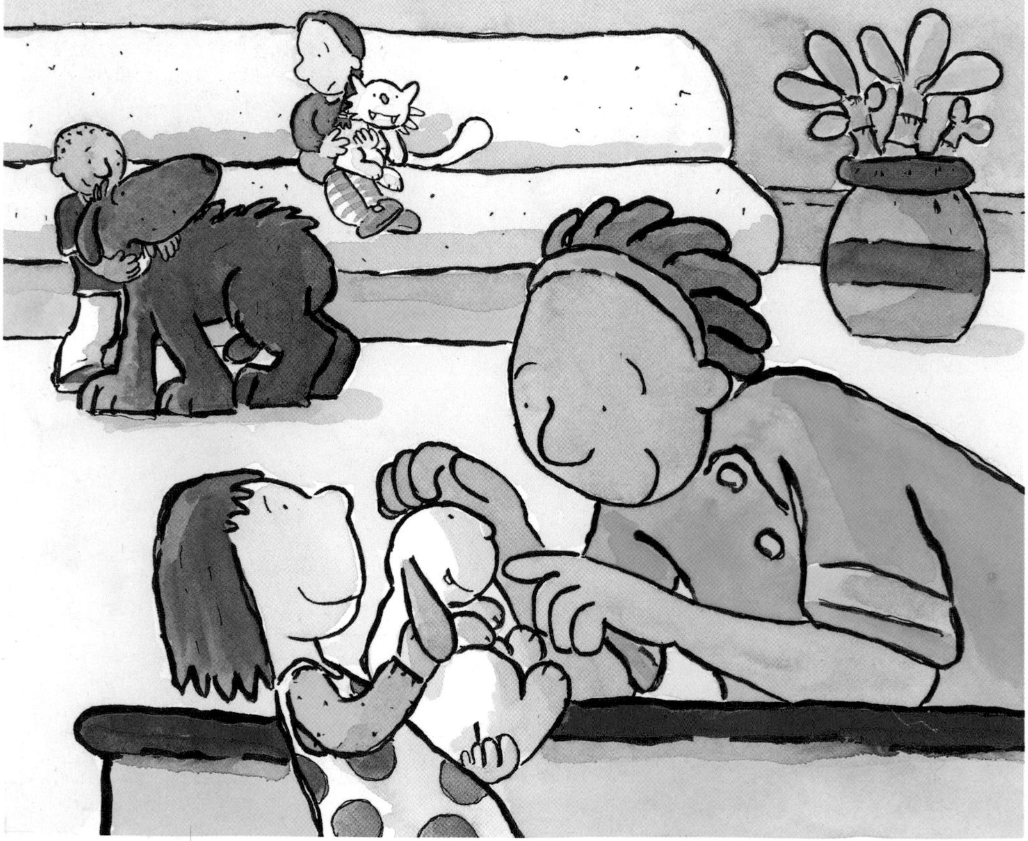

My pet is a rabbit.

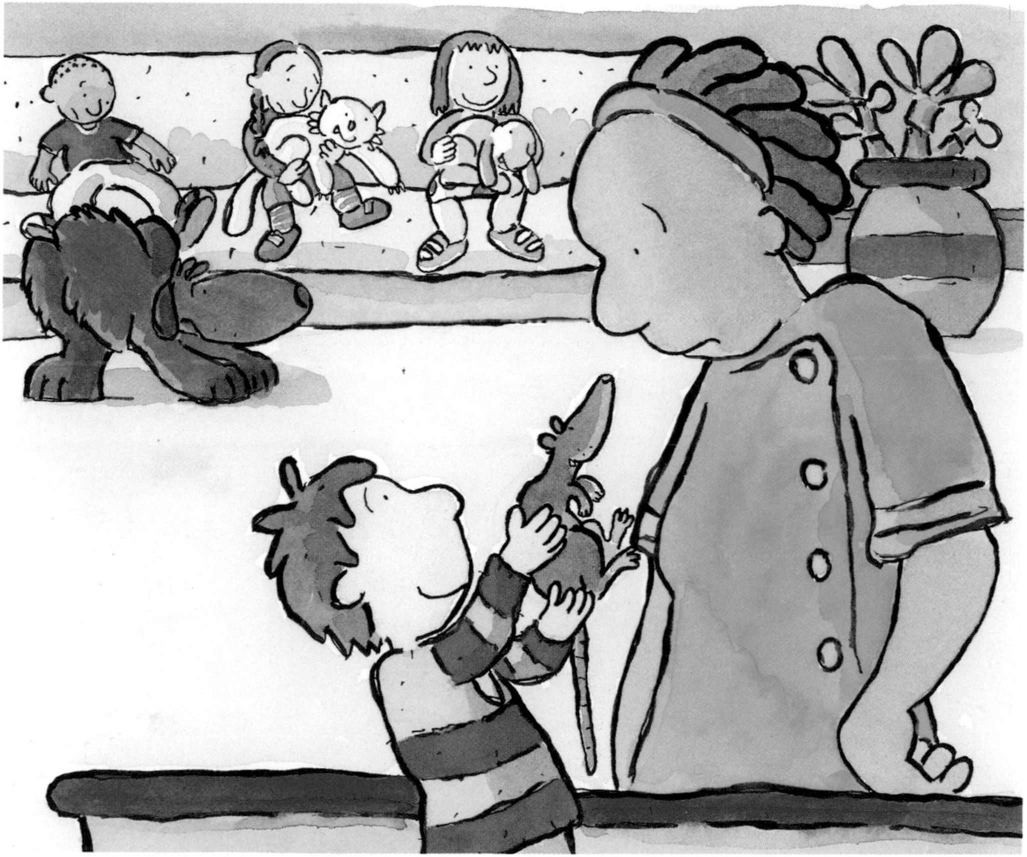

My pet is a rat.

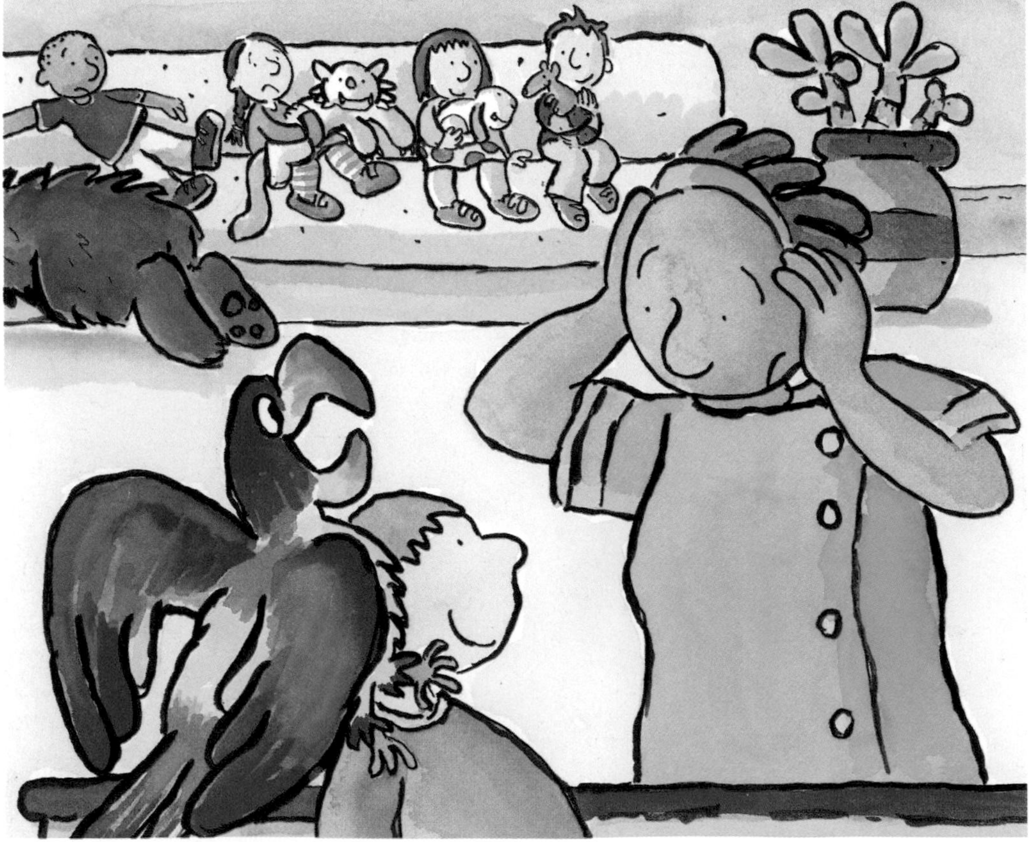

My pet is a parrot.

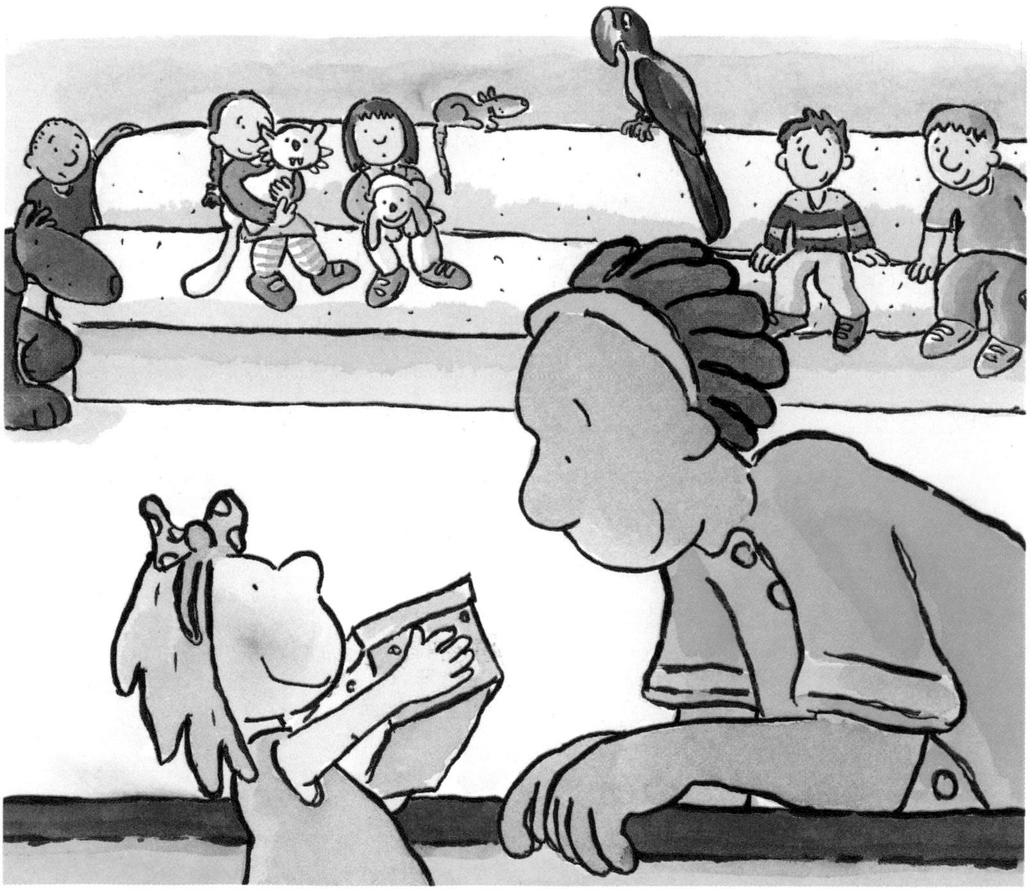

My pet is . . .

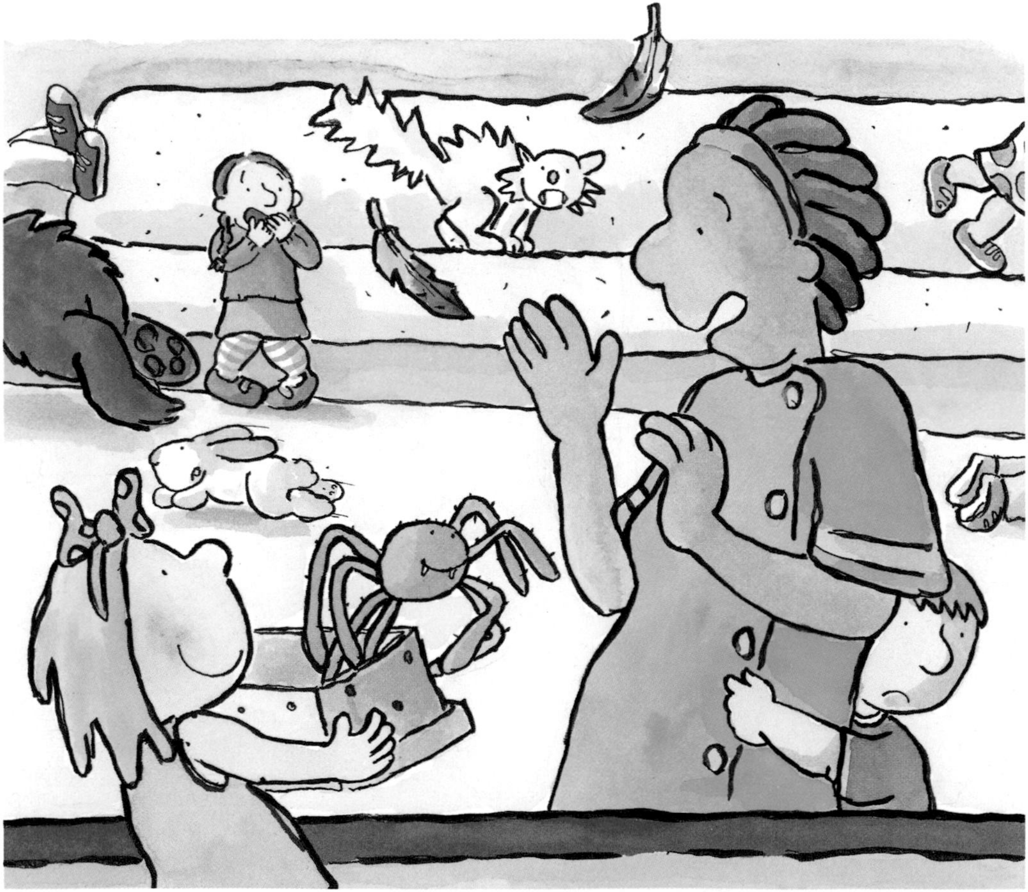

a spider!